# Dig the Dog

Written by
**Alison Maloney**

Illustrated by
**Maddy McClellan**

**meadowside**
CHILDREN'S BOOKS

Dig the Dog dug and dug,
deep down in the dirt.

By the back door,
Dig the Dog buried
a beautiful,
beefy bone.

Doug the Dog dug and dug,
down in the dusty dirt.

Deeper and deeper Doug dug,
under the garden gate.

Doug the Dog
wriggled and wiggled
into the garden
of Dig the Dog.

Dig the Dog was munching and crunching his best bacon biscuits.

# Doug the Dog

sniffed and snuffled
and stuck his snout
in the dirt.

Then he dug and dug,
until he found
the beautiful **beefy** bone.

Then **Doug the Dog** disappeared under the garden gate.

Dig the Dog finished his food and dug in the dirt for dessert.

He snuffled and **Sniffled** and dug and **dug**,

but the beautiful, bone had gone.

Dig the Dog
squeezed and wheezed
under the garden gate.

Doug the Dog was munching and crunching the beautiful beefy bone.

**Dig the Dog** growled and howled and...

...**Doug the Dog** arced and barked.

Doug the Dog
sat and spat

and...

...Dig the Dog
scratched and snatched.

Kit the Cat appeared
and sneered at Dig
and Doug the Dogs.

Doug grinned at Dig.
Dig grinned at Doug.

They raced and chased the Cat.

Kit the Cat
span and ran
as Dig and Doug
barked and larked.

They turned and faced the **beefy** bone.

**Dig the Dog**
licked and Picked.

**Doug the Dog**
chomped and champed.

Until the beautiful **beefy bone...**

...was gone!

For Inigo tiger
and the lovely girls, Mercia, Jo and Melanie.
M.M.

For George Newman
and his brave brother Fred.
A.M.

First Published in 2006
by Meadowside Children's Books
185 Fleet Street
London EC4A 2HS

Text © Alison Maloney
Illustrations © Maddy McClellan
The rights of Alison Maloney and
Maddy McClellan to be identified as the
author and illustrator have been asserted by
them in accordance with the Copyright,
Designs and Patents Act, 1988

A CIP catalogue record for this book
is available from the British Library

ISBN 10 Pbk 1-84539-164-0     ISBN 10 hbk 1-84539-165-9
ISBN 13 Pbk 978-1-84539-164-5  ISBN 13 hbk 978-1-84539-165-2

10 9 8 7 6 5 4 3 2 1
Printed in China